THE
PATCHWORK CAT

Nicola Bayley
& William Mayne

LITTLE GREATS

RANDOM CENTURY

LONDON SYDNEY
AUCKLAND JOHANNESBURG

For Sheila, Doreen and Margaret   W.M.

For John Hilton   N.B.

Text copyright © 1981 William Mayne
Illustrations copyright © 1981 Nicola Bayley
All rights reserved
First published in Great Britain 1981
by Jonathan Cape Ltd
First published in *Little Greats* edition 1991
by Random Century Ltd
20 Vauxhall Bridge Road, London SW1V 2SA

Random Century Australia (Pty) Ltd
20 Alfred Street, Milsons Point, Sydney, NSW 2061

Random Century New Zealand Ltd
PO Box 40-086, Glenfield, Auckland 10, New Zealand

Random Century South Africa (Pty) Ltd
PO Box 337, Bergvlei, 2012, South Africa

Printed in Hong Kong
British Library Cataloguing in Publication Data is available

ISBN 1-85681-182-4

"Good morning, good yawning," says Tabby, getting up. She stretches.

She sleeps on a quilt. It is patch-work, like herself. She loves it.

She loves her breakfast too. She waits for it.

She says good morning, and good yawning to the people who live in her house.

They are a mother and a father and two children.

They all watch for the milkman. Tabby's tail begins to twitch.

They hear his float, they hear him sing.

Tabby goes out and loves the milkman.

"Oh milkman, milkman," she says, "you can come and live at my house any time."

Milk is poured for her.

After breakfast Tabby goes to have another little rest.

But she cannot find the patchwork quilt, her matching, patchwork quilt.

"Ah," says the mother, "we have done some snatchwork on your patchwork. We have thrown it out because it is so very dirty, and we shall buy a basket."

Tabby does not want a basket. She will do some angry scratchwork on it if it comes.

"I think I should send this family away," she says. "I shall have the milkman here to lodge instead."

She goes to look for her
patchwork quilt, to wash herself
and stretch and sleep.

She finds it. It is in the rubbish
bin. She reaches up and touches it.
She climbs in under the lid with it,
and goes to sleep.

Then bang and crash, and black
and thick the dark.

The lid is tightly on, the bin is in the air and upside-down. Tabby falls out, wrapped in her patchwork quilt.

She is in the rubbish truck. She sits and cries with no one there to hear. The engines and the shaking and the dangers and the quaking catch her calls.

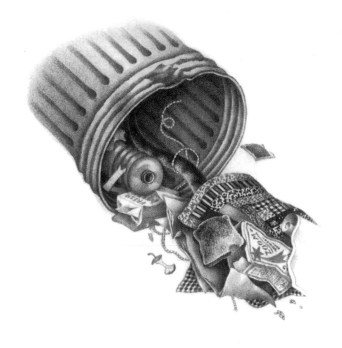

She is going on a journey. She is scared. She does not like it much.

She hisses and she arches up her back, but no one knows.

The journey ends. The truck lifts up its back and hisses. It tips out Tabby and her patchwork quilt.

Where she is she cannot tell. There is nothing good to see and nothing good to smell.

She does not like to touch. She sees that all this place is rubbish. She has to dodge aside, here comes another batch.

And then another, until the day is over. The last truck goes; the driver latches up the gate.

Tabby is in the dump and cannot get out.

She says, "I am a sorry wretch."

Darkness comes. Rats wake up and gnash their teeth at her and flash their eyes.

They watch and make her rage with fright. She guards her patchwork quilt all night, and growls and squalls.

At morning time the rats go home. The gates are opened once again. The trucks begin to pitch the rubbish in.

Tabby drags her patchwork quilt up to the gate. She will not let it go.

She waits until a truck has left, and with her quilt she follows up the track.

She hopes a truck will not come by and crush the patchwork quilt or crunch her bones. She crawls along the ditch.

She holds a corner of the patchwork in her mouth, and has to clench her teeth.

She comes safely out. But she is far from home and does not know how long she'll have to trudge.

She will not go without the patchwork quilt.

Her teeth begin to ache.

She goes along a street and does not know the way. Each turning might be wrong. Which one to take she cannot tell.

She hopes she does not meet a cruel dog or bitch.

Then she hears a sound she knows, and the voice she loves the best. Her tail begins to twitch.

The milkman in his float is there,
the rich voice sings a morning song.

"Good morning," says the
milkman, "here's Tabby far from
home and lost. Come up with me,
and I'll soon fetch you to your
kitchen, with your pretty patchwork quilt that's all the fashion."

Tabby sits beside him on her patchwork quilt, and licks herself.

The milkman pours fresh milk to drink. Tabby is hitch-hiking home.

At home the mother and the father and the children are very pleased to see that she is found.

Tabby thinks that they can stay,
if the milkman will promise to
come each day.

The mother says that she must
wash the patchwork quilt to make it
fresh, and mend it with a stitch or
two to make it new.

Tabby says, "I'll be tired soon,
so wash it now."

When it's clean she sleeps till
dinner time, then wakes and says,
"Good morning, good yawning,"
and has a great big stretch.

She makes sure she is home, and
goes to sleep again all afternoon.